This Land is Your Land

David Clewett

Table of Explorations

Welcome to Cascadia

Cascadia has tremendous history combining natural beauty, fascinating stories, and intriguingly mysterious towns. This book is for the adventurer tired of following the lists of '10 best' later disappointed by an overcrowded endeavor. With expansive wilderness still largely unexplored there is no reason to circle a parking lot for an hour to get a selfie with a beautiful waterfall in the background. Given our rugged history and remarkable scenery we should insist upon feeling a sense of discovery each time we explore.

Hidden deep within our forests are remarkable places that will never appear on a popular tourist list and are left for us to discover. I have long believed that in order to create a worthwhile adventure one must be willing to venture farther than the common traveler.

Initially this project was intended as a guidebook featuring the most incredible secret locations throughout the Pacific Northwest. The undertaking sat idle for years alongside the burden of funding trips to the many places I planned to write about. Even now there are locations I have yet to visit that are worthy of this book. Ultimately there was a realization that becoming an expert on Northwest plants and animals was best left to wildlife biologists.

Eventually I accepted the inability to explain what type of wildflowers grow exclusively along the Metolius River or what birds to look for in the Hoh Rainforest. My ability is describing what it feels like to lay back on a fallen tree while Hemlock Falls' misting reverberations refresh on a summer day. I can describe what it feels like to look up at the Wallowa Mountains and wonder how anything could be more perfect. For those who have never been to Cape

Flattery I am able to explain the feeling of being unable to walk any farther while remaining within these borders.

This book is for my friend Susan Affonso-Malcom and the confidence she expressed for my writing. After many nights of storytelling she asked for a book about my favorite places to explore in the Pacific Northwest.

Below are Susan's words of encouragement:

> You are too kind to give me credit for such a huge task like writing a book. I remember wanting to get to work early just to hear your enthusiasm about this beautiful sanctuary we call home. If I could turn back time we would be exploring this great state together. You have a true gift and your sense of adventure is contagious. You make me want to pack my bags and start from the southern end and work my way north until I've reached every part of this beautiful land. Your family will always come to visit. You need to follow your dreams. You need to find what makes you tick and eat, breathe, and sleep it until you own it. Make paths my friend, where no one else has been and forge ahead. Trust your gut instinct and it will never lead you astray. You're light years ahead of others in your field. The one thing that sets you aside from others is that that there is love written in your words. Love for the state of Oregon. You can do this and I know it will be a hit so much that I will buy the first copy! Now get started while I still have time to read it.

> Susan Affonso-Malcolm
> November 17, 2015

Keep the Gas Tank Full

Travel far and wide.
See mountains, lakes, and rivers,
See eagles soar and grizzlies roar,
See elk, caribou, and moose.

See it all in Washington and Oregon,
See it all in Northern California,
See it all in Idaho's mountainous landscapes,
See it all in Montana and Wyoming.

Wherever you go in the Pacific Northwest,
With a full tank of gas you can see it all.
Travel the backcountry and follow logging roads,
Moving deep into Cascadia's playgrounds.

Stupendous trees grow to stunning heights,
Magnificently clear rivers spring from nothingness,
And critters frolic in their forested kingdoms,
Where water flows and falls in all directions.

The Pacific Northwest is a wonderland,
Where anything dreamed becomes a possibility,
And opportunities are endlessly temping,
With awe-inspiring sights at every turn.

Zen naturalism at its finest with a different climate,
And ecological system every few hundred miles,
From rainforests and coastal environments to the driest,
Most barren and deserted places on the entire planet.

A region rich in forestry, fishing, and environmentalism,
Tall and rugged mountain peaks to low canyons,
Severe elevation changes and volcanic history,
Resulting in the deepest, bluest lakes in the world.

It can all be seen in the mythical land of Cascadia,
Where nymphs and legends roam the forests,
And the stories of our early ancestors sing onward,
In breaking waves, breezy winds, and gurgling streams.

Washington:

"Earth and sky, woods and fields, lakes and rivers, the mountain and the sea, are excellent schoolmasters, and teach some of us more than we can ever learn from books."

John Lubbock

Falls Creek Falls: Carson, WA

Turn your head,
Crane your neck.
Look up to the Falls,
Marvel at their omnipotence.

Supreme power and authority,
Over the rocks, soil, and earth,
As water carries everything in its path,
Over the edge landing in the pool below.

Look up at the Falls,
And wonder of those,
Who have stood here before,
Hearing this deafening noise.

Close your eyes and listen.
Imagine the waterfall before you.
It never existed,
Before you pictured water flowing.

Let the water purify your mind,
Offering clarity and calming your being.
Envision the water flowing down upon you,
Over your body and gently cleansing your soul.

Take a seat on a rock,
Take a seat on a log,
Settle at the pew,
At the Temple of the Falls.

Sit patiently beneath,
These wondrous waters.
Cross your legs and fold your hands,
Appreciate the perceived falls before you.

With eyes closed –
Imagine the rainbow,
And the bright green moss.
Hear the ancient wisdom of stories and lessons.

Lift your head with eyes still closed,
Visualize the falls and all their details,
The magnificent show as water flows,
Through your peaceful imagination.

Be quiet and simply observe,
Silently take in the scene before you,
Learn from this natural phenomenon,
Fold your hands and achieve dhyana.

Deep Lake: Colville, WA

This is what Kerouac was chasing –
Solitude in the mountains at the Canadian border,
With only nature, his own musings, notepads,
A book or two, and memories as entertainment.

Now, it is his journey that I chase –
Following closely in his footsteps.
Cherishing the same simple pleasures,
Tracing his route and the trails he traveled.

Located amid the Aladdin Valley and Colville National,
Deep Lake sits serenely among remote wilderness,
Where the Selkirk and Kettle ranges host rare wildlife,
Including the woodland caribou, grizzly, moose, and lynx.

Deep Lake –

As the day comes to a close,
Steam rises from beneath the hillside trees,
A heavy moisture in the air fills the cool evening,
While birds begin feeding feverishly near the shores.

Dim lights illuminate the few small cabins,
Casting long misshapen shadows,
Across the length of the calm water,
Creating an eerie perception of population.

The whistling of birds in nearby trees,
And small ripples caused by rising fish,
Are all that remind me that I am not alone,
Having companions in this isolated location.

Deep Lake –

With your soggy rain soaked trees,
Dripping into your glacial waters,
These mysteriously green forests protect,
The wisdom Kerouac discovered here.

Stillness, in perfect quietude and tranquility.
As the day closes and the sun disappears,
Behind your western tree line in perfection,
A grey wolf lets out a final howl and I am in love.

Skagit River: Marblemount, WA

I would come down from the mountains,
Along a trail I had carved through the forest,
To enjoy the river at least one night every week.

The trail led to the small town of Marblemount,
And I would emerge from the subalpine forest,
On the backside of the community General Store.

After purchasing a bottle of Washington wine,
I'd make a quick scamper across the highway,
And find my way down to the Skagit River.

Perched atop a boulder I could smell the water,
And feel the forceful rush of its heaving bulk,
While sitting cross-legged underneath the starry sky.

With meditative sips I'd drink the wine poor boy style,
While occasionally puffing on my pipe and scribbling,
With my #2 pencil in a Golden West notebook.

The Skagit is a powerful and fertile mountain river,
Moving entire mountains unlike any other,
Carrying with it logs, rocks, and soil downhill.

At Marblemount, the river surges with the Cascade,
Emerging with greater purpose and forming a dull green,
That is unlike any other color naturally found in the world.

I would sit on the banks until well after midnight,
Gazing upward and drinking to the sizzle of the stars,
Mesmerized by glittering moonlight on spectacular water.

There by the Skagit –
My favorite river in all of Washington,

I'd emerge from the forest at night and drink.

Composing a few do-nothing haikus,
In gratefulness and gratitude,
For this contemplative North Cascades River.

Beacon Rock: Stevenson, WA

Mighty Columbia come roaring down,
Like a rushing bull passing the matador safely on shore,
Flow past the silhouetted Beacon in the fading light.
With her outstretched muleta to charge beneath,

Great Columbia River continue your journey,
Onward over the Bonneville toward the wide open sea.
Carry on past the Beacon along your thousand mile voyage,
Guiding explorers westward to the Pacific Ocean.

To Astoria and the Graveyard of the Columbia,
Where thousands of ships have wrecked at the bar,
Due to unpredictable weather, current, and waves,
And undoubtedly the wrath of Colossal Claude.

The Beacon observes at all times,
From the north shore keeping watch,
During torrential storms and on warm summer days,
Through all the seasons from its high vantage point.

The pinnacle of the Columbia functions as a lighthouse,
Guiding fishermen to safety as they navigate the waterway,
Providing a directional waypoint in the fog and chop,
So that all may find their way when the waters get rough.

Known as Che-Che-op-tin or 'Navel of the World,'
The Native People considered Beacon the belly-button,
And the historically iconic basalt column is the remains,
Of an ancient volcano that survived the Missoula Floods.

Lewis and Clark's campground on their way to the Pacific,
They stopped in 1805 and gave name to the uppermost,
Indicator of tidal influence along the Columbia River,
And the name Beaten Rock persisted for many years.

The great natural marigraph of the Pacific,
Letting people 120 miles away from the mouth,
Keep accurate records of the changing tides,
With Beacon as their trusted measuring tool.

It is home to nesting falcons,
Perched high upon the cliffs of the rock,
With the supreme vantage point,
For hunting smaller birds that feed below.

At the top, a wide panoramic view of the Gorge awaits,
Breathtaking spectacle of the bisecting Columbia,
With the Bonneville Dam and its thundering ruckus,
Just upstream as the great tamer of this mighty river.

Devils Tower, Stone Mountain, and El Capitan,
Get their fair share of publicity as national icons.
But Beacon Rock has reason to claim recognition,
As the Northwest's notably prominent monolith.

All who climb to the top of Beacon Rock,
Are indebted in gratitude for H. Biddle's efforts,
Saving the pillar from demolition and instead,
Blasting a switch-backing trail right up the side.

Beacon of the Columbia,
Lighthouse of this forever immense river,
Stand tall and distinguished for eternity,
Keeping watchful eye over all in the Gorge.

Grand Coulee Dam: Electric City, WA

The magnificent Grand Coulee Dam,
Brought life to the Pacific Northwest.
A remarkable feat of engineering so significant,
Roosevelt attended the grand opening ceremony.

The most phenomenal achievement of mankind,
To harness the power of America's great river,
But it would take just the shoulder of a Native woman,
For the floodwaters to be freely swallowed by the salmon.

With just a simple nudge that majestic salmon,
Now waiting in the Pacific could swim upstream,
Through the Columbia to the mouth of the Spokane,
Once again in its native spawning grounds.

Man's most remarkable feat of engineering,
Utilizing the power of the mighty Columbia River,
Had one predominantly glaring oversight in its planning,
By not including a ladder for salmon to get upstream.

For centuries salmon ran freely year-after-year,
From the Pacific Ocean up the Columbia to spawn,
And the Colville people fished them along the journey,
Catching an abundance at Kettle Falls to feed their families.

While Roosevelt and others observed the finished dam,
Native People from all over the region gathered,
At Kettle Falls one last time to say farewell,
With many tribes joining in a Ceremony of Tears.

Manifest Destiny was rolling through the west,
And dreams of lush farmlands with plenty of water,
Surpassed rational thinking for the lives of Native People,
While sacrificing the once fertile salmon spawning waters.

But the Grand Coulee was a miraculous feat,
To harness nature's power and improve the land,
And the livelihood for many throughout the west,
So they could thrive in an otherwise challenging climate.

The misty crystal glitter of that wild windward spray,
Was set aside for irrigation, shipping, and electricity,
To help the common white man working a farm,
And sustain a suitable lifestyle fitting for his kind.

Many men fought the pounding waters,
Met a watery grave in the construction of Grand Coulee.
The Columbia tore boats to splinters fighting back,
As the Dam grew across her great spread waters.

The New Deal brought electricity out west,
And the mightiest thing ever built by man,
It provided food and prosperity for many,
By controlling the mightiest thing ever built by nature.

Roll on, Columbia.
Roll on and break down these man-made barriers.
Flood the cities and rush freely to the Pacific.
Reunite the salmon and Native People at Kettle Falls.

North Cascades National Park: Diablo, WA

The rucksack generation thrives here.
Those of us wandering the jagged,
Rough terrain of the North Cascades,
Knapsacks on our backs and notepads in hand.

We are Zen Lunatics on the mountain peaks.
Who climb as high up as our legs will take us,
Then look down below and write poems,
As fast as they storm into the *vijñāna*.

We preach eternal freedom.
Sharing the wisdom of the mountains,
With those we meet along the trail,
While climbing farther to remote vistas.

For us there is no place superior.
A certain majestic mountain scenery,
With snowfields, glaciers, alpine meadows, and lakes,
Providing inspiration unlike any other natural scenery.

No one thing in life gives such unalloyed pleasure,
As simply being in the mountains.
Seeing the world as the mind's invention,
Becoming rivers, sun, flies, and stars.

Enough time in the North Cascades,
And you will forget things once read.
Become entirely captured by the morning fog,
Rising up to reveal Ross Lake below.

The rocky terrain here is only for the serious poet,
With rucksacks on our backs and courageous souls,
We climb to the most remote peaks of North Cascades,
Returning home with Zen and a yearning for nirvana.

Panther Creek Falls: Carson, WA

An amphitheater suitable even for John Muir,
With the most tranquil solitude found anywhere.
Gently cascading water produces the only sound,
As it eases quietly into Big Huckleberry Creek.

Water moves in a more domesticated manner here,
Leaving the tumultuous roaring falls to the Gorge.
Panther Creek travels majestically and gracefully,
Softly gliding over the earthly green mossy face.

A most complex waterfall with deep grooves,
Steering the spate creating gullies and channels,
With the creek divulging into several small streams,
Over a two tiered plunge to the rocky pool below.

A series of springs spewing water from earth create,
Spilling rivulets that trickle over the moss-covered wall,
And a dramatic scene of multi-faceted cascades,
That are overwhelmingly surreal to the senses.

A nearby rope tied securely to a large stump,
Leads to a moss-topped platform and the creek below,
Where the full amphitheater is given perspective,
And the many misty glistening falls are observable.

This clandestine cascade of the Gifford Pinchot,
With concealed gardens and multitude of colors,
May be the most mesmerizing of all the falls,
Throughout the entire Pacific Northwest.

A series of surprises just waiting for discovery,
Hidden alongside a logging road deep in the forest.
With minimal signage the entire experience feels,
Like unearthing a multitude of long lost treasures.

Bridge of the Gods: North Bonneville, WA

When the people of the region had difficulties,
Navigating around the immense Columbia River,
Manito built a bridge from earth and stone for them,
And placed the elderly Loowit as its trusted guardian.

Formed from the Bonneville landslide,
That dammed the river creating a natural bridge,
When the lava cliffs of Table Mountain,
And the north wall of the Columbia Gorge fell.

The Bridge stood 300 feet above water level,
So that Native Americans could cross the river,
Aiding in their fishing and hunting efforts,
While making an inland sea of the Columbia.

The natural stone Tamanawas Bridge was destroyed,
When Squaw Mountain emerged between Klickitat,
And Wyeast creating an epic environmental love triangle,
Where the two brothers feuded over Squaw Mountain.

The rivalry boiled over when Klickitat and Wyeast,
Began hurling white-hot rocks, setting fire to forests,
Spatting ashes, and belching black smoke in their rage,
Until their fury collapsed the Bridge of the Gods.

Loowit tried to stop the fight but eventually fell,
Into the newly created rapids where the bridge once stood.
She had a bleak outlook before being granted a final wish,
And was turned into the *beautiful* Mount St. Helens.

This battle between brothers is commonly called,
The Great Cascadia Subduction Zone earthquakes,
Which in the 1690s released the river to flow freely,
Making the expansive Columbia impassable once again.

Two centuries later a new Bridge of the Gods,
Was constructed stretching across the Columbia,
Connecting Washington's SR-14 at Skamania,
With Oregon's I-84 to the south at Cascade Locks.

Now the Bridge serves as an economic resource,
Making commerce available throughout the Gorge,
And is perhaps best known as the lowest point,
On the famed and preeminent Pacific Crest Trail.

Thousands of day hikers pass over the bridge every year,
And hundreds of through hikers gather provisions,
Before crossing the bridge on the final leg of their journey,
Enjoying the scenic northbound welcome to Washington.

Tremendous views on both sides crossing the Columbia,
Bridge of the Gods is an experience of remembrance,
Bringing forth centuries of history in only a few minutes,
Traversing the same sacred route of Tamanawas Bridge.

Hoh Rainforest: Forks, WA

No canopy more opaque than the Hoh Rainforest,
Where rain cannot even reach the damp soil beneath,
Without first resting in the depressed leaves of the trees,
Before slowly dripping and descending to the forest floor.

The region is like an altogether different world,
A temperate forest where rain always falls,
With coniferous and deciduous species,
Enveloped in a mess of moss and fern.

A magical ecosystem comparable to Rivendell,
With moss covered trees and streams gently flowing,
Through the enchanted forest of lush greenery,
Situated on the western edge of the Olympic Peninsula.

The clear and undammed Hoh River passes through,
Hosting one of the healthiest wild salmon runs in the US,
With the Hoh Tribe looking over the river from its mouth,
And overseeing all activity within Olympic National Park.

Originating from the Hoh Glacier at Mount Olympus,
The river flows 56 miles to the mouth at the Pacific,
Where for centuries the Hoh People have guarded,
Against stranded naval explorers attempting to invade.

The Sitka spruce and western hemlock grow tall,
And lettuce lichen thrive in the moist conditions,
Where beneath the canopy of old growth forests,
Deer and elk stroll unnoticed in the undergrowth.

The Hoh Rainforest is a wonderfully eerie location.
Its congested and impenetrable density combined,
With a remote and desolate location creates uneasiness,
Making the feeling of claustrophobia remarkably profound.

A beautiful ecosystem in the secluded northwest,
Sopped and soaking in soggily stunning terrain,
The Hoh Rainforest of the Olympic is a dramatic sight,
Uniquely found in only a few places throughout the world.

Desolation Peak: North Cascades, WA

Just a small, wooden, one room structure equipped,
With a wood stove, small cot, and panoramic views,
Of the North Cascades near the Canadian border,
Overlooking miles of forested mountains and alpine lakes.

Atop Desolation Peak with fifteen miles to the nearest road,
This is remote even in the most far-off parts of Cascadia,
And anyone intent on visiting the lookout must traverse,
Steep trail with only the views as motive to push onward.

A place where one can scan the scene in solitude,
Stop the machine of thinking and meet spirits of place,
Lie in the grass or sit on a rock and look up at the clouds,
Simply grateful for time to enjoy the pure act of living.

At six thousand feet this feels like the top of the world,
Where fields explode with paintbrush and lupine.
Entrancing views of Ross Lake and Sourdough,
Provide plenty enough for a Dharma poet to meditate.

With Hozomeen's twin peaks as nearest neighbor,
One could proclaim from a first-awed glimpse,
It was the most stunningly flawless mountain ever seen,
With its Dharmakaya immensely untouchable towers.

No setting more ideal for studying the Diamond Sutra,
With intent upon conditioning the mind to emptiness,
Becoming a factory for writing - churning word-after-word,
Filling pages and notebooks with stories of past adventures.

Seeking Prajna-samadhi of Hui-Neng on Vulture Peak.
But then, with peaceful solitude comes a strong yearning,
For drugs and liquor to accelerate the desired visions,

Instead of the empty barren fatalism of mountaintop.

Returning from Desolation without a magical vision,
But bursting with memories of a most recent adventure.
Departing as a *Dharma Bum* toward next destination,
Prepared to fill journals with tales from The Lookout.

Diablo Lake: North Cascades, WA

Nestled among the North Cascades alpine scenery,
The Skagit is dammed to form a turquoise colored lake,
Surrounded on all sides by snow covered peaks,
Including Jack, Sourdough, Colonel, Pyramid, and Davis.

Sourdough is why I am here alongside Blackie Burns,
To watch the changing mood over vast landscapes,
Light moving with the day and the countless clouds,
The towering cumulous above with Diablo down below.

An unmistakable green hue created by mountain glaciers,
That grind rocks to a glacial flour that flows into the lake,
Carried by creeks to give the water an inimitable tint,
Resonating in the flat calm waters affront tall peaks.

Rough terrain of mountain summits make appreciable,
The risky elevation of this North Cascades lake.
Steep and narrow switchbacks make me wish for a horse,
With Willy the Paint's grace to travel this alpine terrain.

Standing among the wildflowers of a south-facing meadow,
The sinuous green of the Skagit reappears with Diablo,
And the indistinct ripple of a tour boat 4,000 feet below,
As it moves past forested islands in the middle of the lake.

Climbing onward up Pierce Mountain Trail,
Sourdough sits with a smoky sky in the backdrop,
And expansive views of the east side of the valley,
From Jack to Desolation and the crags of Hozomeen.

A sweet and beautiful environment atop Sourdough,
With wet and grassy green meadows filled with color,
And the essence of wildflowers throughout the summer,
Creating a wonderful heavenly landscape to explore.

With D.T. Suzuki in hand and *Walden* in my pocket,
The views down to Diablo Lake are surreally mesmerizing.
Captivating the mind for hours of reading and meditation,
Watching mountains shift around the magnificent lake.

Batsquatch: Mount St. Helens, WA

The flying cryptid of Mount St. Helens,
A primate with wings akin to Ahool,
Yellow-eyed with a wolf-like muzzle,
Nine feet tall with sharp teeth and bird feet.

Batsquatch spawned from the eruption of St. Helens,
Which unleashed catastrophic destruction throughout,
Leaving an enormous crater atop the flattened mountain,
And setting the winged beast free to roam the forests.

When the dust settled those in the area began reporting,
A humanoid creature with glowing eyes lurking around,
The areas of destruction and emanating an intense feeling,
Of dread and sinister maleficence in the region.

Batsquatch is an imposing figure with wingspan,
Upwards of fifty feet and the ability to affect cars,
Most famously stopping Brian Canfield's truck in 1994,
On a remote road in dark wilderness near Lake Kapowsin.

The report confirmed the creature had expanded its range,
And as Canfield's brand new truck stopped unexpectedly,
He sat in the fading daylight with the motor running,
But the truck refused to move despite all logical rationale.

Suddenly something glided in front of his headlights,
Soaring like an aircraft coming in for a landing,
Stared straight at Canfield while spreading its wings,
Then showed its teeth before moving on to a nearby field.

A few minutes later the truck slowly idled forward,
And Canfield drove away with trembling fingers.
His heart raced and he frantically drove to Camp One,
Where he reported the story to his waiting friends.

Also in 1994 a pilot named Butch Whittaker reported,
That a similar creature to the one Canfield encountered,
Flew up next to his aircraft soaring above Mt. Rainier,
And kept pace with the small plane before flying away.

In 1998 near Mt. Rainier a log truck struck a Batsquatch,
And a responding witness observed the vehicle,
Steering off the road down a cliff and afterward,
Saw a wingspread triumphant Batsquatch atop the hood.

The demon monster born out of Loowits' eruption,
Batsquatch roams the remote forests of Washington,
And has affinity for striking vehicles without warning,
With a degree of potential destruction unknown to us all.

Port Townsend, WA

At the northeast tip of the Olympic Peninsula sits a town,
With Victorian buildings dating to the late 19th century,
When Port Townsend was the 'City of Dreams' seaport,
Intent on becoming the largest harbor on the west coast.

The prosperous settlement was developed almost overnight,
With a heyday of buildings and homes constructed,
To support plans for a booming shipping port,
And a major city already showing signs of growth.

The Long Depression hit and railway plans halted,
Town declined quickly as the boom was over.
Without the railroad to spur economic growth,
People began moving and investing elsewhere.

The rapid boom then bust of the town preserved,
Victorian architecture on the hilly slopes alongside,
A Carnegie Library, Courthouse, Fort Worden,
And a one-of-a-kind bell tower for calling firefighters.

Maritime life and boating provide an anchor for industry,
With many classic wooden boats calling the port home,
Like Steinbeck's 'The Western Flyer' made famous by,
His voyage to Mexico and *The Log from the Sea of Cortez*.

Over 300 Victorian-style homes remain in Port Townsend,
Elegant and ornate mansions with scenic coastal views,
And the snow-capped Olympic Mountains in the distance,
Only briefly enjoyed by wealthy merchants and captains.

Near the Strait of Juan de Fuca the historic town,
Continues to persevere as a thriving arts community,
But the significance of the area preserved through time,
Makes Port Townsend a notably picturesque discovery.

Cadborosaurus: Henry Island, WA

Lurking off the northern coast of Washington,
Is a horse-headed serpent up to fifty feet long,
Reportedly with a series of humps and a long neck,
With gray-brown-green skin, vertical coils, and flippers.

The monster has been seen since the 1700s,
And is commonly referenced in American Indian folklore,
With sightings and accounts throughout history,
And among memories of those in the Pacific Northwest.

In the 1930s Cadborosaurus was seen by many onlookers,
At Neah Bay on the tip of the Olympic Peninsula.
When Caddy ate a duck floating on the water in 1934,
Duck hunters near Waldron Island were watching.

In 1936 a twelve foot Caddy washed ashore at Aberdeen,
And scientists quickly attempted to study the specimen,
But the remains had mostly rotted leaving very little,
And not enough evidence to definitely classify.

Caddy was photographed in 1937 by a group of fishermen,
Who found a twenty-foot carcass in a sperm whale,
But the remains were too decomposed for identification,
And scientists did not feel confident confirming the picture.

In 1953 two women saw Caddy near Port Townsend,
At the Strait of Juan de Fuca as it partially emerged,
Revealing ten foot long stretches of its enormous body,
With a flat head and six foot long giraffe-like neck.

A baby Caddy was found on a San Juan Islands beach,
In 1991 by Phyllis Harsh who described the creature,
As a 'baby dinosaur' that she gently pushed with a stick,
Until watching the serpent swim back out to sea.

Most recently in 2009 a fisherman filmed a Caddy,
Swimming with its head emerged and long body,
Twisting up and out of the water as it propelled,
Which is best proof toward the validity of the monster.

There's no doubt about the great serpent of the northwest,
As so much evidence and eye-witness reports all match.
While the creature has been unproven for centuries,
It is only a matter of time before the species is confirmed.

Raymond, WA

Upon first sight the most perfect town in America.
With logs piled high and plentiful along the Willapa,
And the smell of fresh caught fish permeating the salty air.
Historic buildings create mystery of past and present.

Inland from the mouth of Willapa River at the Pacific,
And at the inlet of Willapa Bay in Southwest Washington,
Raymond is the model industrial town where hard work,
Provides the lifestyle cherished by many in the Northwest.

Situated just off State Route 101 in North Pacific County,
The persevering town boasts logging and fishing,
As economic drivers but it is the scenic views,
That makes 'The City That Does Things' so remarkable.

The town was originally built with elevated sidewalks,
And raised streets to connect buildings on stilts,
Above tidelands and sloughs that crisscrossed the site,
Of the once wild and wooly lumber mill and fishing town.

Historic buildings such as the 1928 Raymond Theatre,
Provide appeal for this charming little community,
On the Cranberry Coast of Washington where steamboats,
Still navigate through the shallow waters of Willapa Bay.

Home to an incredible collection of antique vehicles,
Including 19th century carriages, buggies, and wagons.
Steel sculptures of wildlife and people adorn the sidewalks,
Enlivening the appealing heritage of this unique area.

Raymond has claim to Nirvana's first ever performance,
The beginning of grunge at a house party in March 1987,
Though the community is satisfied being largely unnoticed,
Out of the way left to enjoy simple pleasures and beauty.

With piles of fresh cut logs stacked neatly along the river,
And boats actively fishing or loading supplies for transport.
On a summer day this town oozes old world industrialism,
Preserving a bygone era with pride in a day of hard work.

Winthrop, WA

Rising from the Methow Valley in North Central WA,
Settled alongside the Methow River on the Cascade Loop,
Winthrop provides wonder as the North Cascades loom,
And the world turns back into an old west cowboy town.

With the discovery of placer gold in 1868,
Settlers began arriving in Winthrop including Guy Waring,
The acclaimed founding father of the small mountain town,
Whose original Duck Brand Saloon remains as Town Hall.

Although Waring founded the town it is the gifted author,
And Union Civil War officer Theodore Winthrop,
Who received remembrance as namesake for the town,
After his literature was published posthumously to acclaim.

The town's real heroes are Kathryn and Otto Wagner,
The visionary duo sought to save the burgeoning town,
Capitalizing on tourism and the newly opened highway 20,
And in the 1960s converted businesses to their origins.

Now walking the streets of this unique settlement,
Feels like stepping back into the old west where miners,
Would have walked the streets for supplies and taverns,
With their horses tied to nearby hitching posts outside.

It is a town of wonder and awe where life moves slower,
Cars quickly become burdensome as the wood sidewalks,
Are the preferred method for seeing each building,
In the town preserved for the remembrance of history.

Akin to genuine old west towns in the Southwest,
Preserved like Tombstone, Jerome, and Winslow,
The recreation captures the feeling of John McCabe,
In the mining town of Presbyterian Church in 1902.

A picturesque piece of history on the edge of adventure,
Winthrop provides scenery of the nearby North Cascades,
From a historical settlement that exhibits old west charm,
With the ever present serenading sounds of Methow River.

Leavenworth, WA

A small mountain village in North Central Washington,
Where the buildings resemble the German town of Bavaria,
And the community lives up to the reputation best they can,
Creating an authentic experience in the Pacific Northwest.

It is a small steep country more vertical than sideways,
With large brown hotels built on the cuckoo clock style,
Where storefronts release an aroma of baked goods,
High up in alpine country along the Wenatchee River.

Modeled with faceted buildings and two-toned timber,
Houses and shops reminiscent those in the German Alps,
The town boasts merriment and festivities comparable,
Of its German likeness true to architecture and charm.

The once thriving logging town headquartered,
The Great Northern Railway in the early 1900s,
Until the railroad relocated and the community entered,
A period of struggle without the means to ship timber.

Leavenworth was reinvented in the 1960s to support,
A tourism industry that would bring people far and wide,
To see the Northwest's German style Bavarian village,
And the outdoor recreation of the surrounding region.

Nearby Blackbird Island is a peaceful natural area,
With the sound of birds calling and fish rising,
As the Wenatchee River rolls by with deer and wildlife,
Passing regularly along the many trail systems.

Icicle River drains the Wenatchee National Forest,
From the crest of the Cascade Range at Josephine Lake,
Forming as a shallow clear stream that glides peacefully,
Holding massive salmon in its cold glacial waters.

Back in town people walk the streets and explore shops,
Sampling food or drinking in the many German-style pubs,
Until nightfall when the city lights create a different aura,
And the magical scenery makes a perfect setting for love.

Cape Flattery: Neah Bay, WA

Leaning against the rail is not advised.
There are certain boundaries put in place,
And this one ends abruptly and ultimately marks,
The northwestern-most point in the contiguous U.S.

An entire continent ends definitively,
Marked by rugged steep cliffs with lush forest,
Views of Makah Bay and Neah Bay surrounding,
The lookouts vantage of low rocky islands and sea caves.

With the Fuca Pillar and various land mass islands rising,
And the distant Tatoosh Island resembling Alcatraz,
The scene is tremendous from the point toward the sea,
With Flattery a most modest moniker for this cape.

Named by Captain James Cook in 1778 the cape pleased,
Even his most distinguished tastes and expertise in travel,
And his proclamation stuck making Cape Flattery,
The oldest permanently named location in Washington.

The Cape emerges from a lush coastal forest,
Of western red-cedar, Sitka spruce, and western hemlock,
With a boggy thicket of salmonberry growing throughout,
And views of Kessiso Rocks along the journey.

Calling themselves kwih-dich-chuh-ahtx meaning,
'The people who live by the rocks and seagulls,'
The Makah have lived near Neah Bay four millennia,
In a small fishing village along the Pacific Ocean.

They have long hunted seals and humpback whales,
Along with harvesting shellfish and forests for food,
And still continue the tradition of aboriginal whaling,
Using harpoons to kill the whale from cedar canoes.

Chief Tatoosh is remembered in his island namesake,
Which was inhabited seasonally by Makah fishing camps.
Now vacant aside from the dormant Cape Flattery Light,
It is home to nesting seabirds and marine mammals.

Hundreds of sea stacks line this undisturbed coastline,
With abundant wildlife viewed from the rocky cliffs,
Including sea lions basking on Snake Rock and puffins,
Guillemots, and Murres nesting on the precipices below.

The crashing waves provide ample reminder,
That with each strike the cape moves just a little,
South and slightly east as the land chisels away,
Reducing mass with each and every tidal change.

Without the ability to travel any further north or west,
The feeling at Cape Flattery is one of limitless limitations.
The boundary is definitive within the continental confines,
Yet the expansive views create wonder of more to explore.

Loowitlatkla: Cougar, WA

Mount St. Helens gurgles, boils, and trembles,
Spitting out the occasional plume of fiery lava,
As the Puyallup Tribe observes minor tremors,
In the furiously active mountain ready to burst.

It was a regular occurrence for Northwest Natives,
Ever since the landslide filled the Columbia creating,
A natural stone bridge providing safe crossing of the river,
And the sacred Tamanawas Bridge became a destination.

Tribes from all around the region traveled far and wide,
To collect embers from a small fire perpetually burning,
Known to be the only fire that existed in the entire world,
Tended by Loowitlatkla at the center of Bridge of the Gods.

A wrinkled old woman who lived at the center of the arch,
Loowit was faithful to her task providing embers to tribes,
So they could start fires elsewhere for their people.
Her efforts were recognized by the Great Chief Sahale.

The Chief had previously granted eternal life to his sons,
Klickitat and Wyeast and offered the same gift to Loowit,
But she did not want to live forever as an old woman,
So he granted her eternal youth and wondrous beauty.

When Wyeast came from the Multnomah's to see Loowit,
And Klickitat stormed in from the north to meet him,
Both brothers fell in love with the beautiful woman,
And in their battle Tamanawas Bridge fell into the river.

As punishment for their feud and damage caused to forests,
Wyeast was smote but maintained pride as Mount Hood,
Klickitat's sorrow reflected in the bend of Mount Adams,
And Loowit became a most beautiful symmetrical cone.

The Lady of Fire erupted in 1980 diminishing her charm,
But she boils on actively along the Cascade Range,
Not entirely dormant and still aching for the love,
Of Wyeast and Klickitat in her urge for youthful beauty.

Oregon:

"I must walk toward Oregon, and not toward Europe. And that way the nation is moving, and I may say that mankind progress from east to west. We go eastward to realize history and study the works of art and literature, retracing the steps of the race; we go westward as into the future, with a spirit of enterprise and adventure."

Henry David Thoreau

Blacklock Point: Langlois, OR

Rolling knolls of grassy green promontory,
Highlighted by vibrant wildflowers on hillside bluffs,
Vivid colors and the aroma of purple, yellow, and orange,
With Western Trillium and Blue Flag sacredly scattered.

An exposed natural embankment guarded,
By thickets of damp sheltered coastal woodland,
Ultimately ceding to undiscovered shorelines,
Revealing secret and protected remote beaches.

Vast and expansive untouched coastline,
Polluted only by driftwood and seaweed,
With castle-like sea stacks anchored in the waves,
Views of Cape Blanco Lighthouse to the south.

Westernmost of all that is west,
Jutting out to the farthest reaches,
Closest of all to the setting sun,
With perfect driftwood seats for the view.

The Tufted Puffin choose wisely,
And nest in crevices of nearby rocks.
The sweeping sea gives cold kisses to my toes,
Greeting them as if it were the first time.

This undisturbed gemstone of the Pacific,
Where the hills are alive and their music,
Can be found in the sound of the crashing waves,
Provides electrifying stimulation to the wandering soul.

Requiring sufficient effort to locate and reveal,
A magical discovery hidden along the coastline.
One of the best kept secrets in the Pacific Northwest,
Where the naturalism of Cascadia remains unspoiled.

Sixes River: Sixes, OR

Meandering thirty-one miles down a lush valley,
Draining a rugged region of the Klamath Mountains,
Eventually rising in the coastal range of Curry County,
Just south of Sugarloaf heading west toward the Pacific.

Sixes River flows through the Grassy Knob Wilderness,
And the wonderfully remote coastal community of Sixes,
Before emerging near Cape Blanco and Blacklock Point,
Ultimately pouring into the Pacific at Castle Rock.

From the Historic Hughes House the Sixes can be viewed,
At the mouth of the Pacific with natural landscape.
Rolling hills previously used to raise cattle and grow crops,
Creates a remarkable view that is almost unimaginable.

The Queen Anne-style home of Port Orford Cedar,
Built by local contractor Pehr Johan Lindberg in 1898,
Housed members of the Hughes family until 1971,
And still stands largely unaltered along the coastline.

Gold found the Sixes in 1856 bringing Patrick Hughes,
And a flurry of others to settle near the south coast river,
With their riches in sight sweeping along the rocky bottom,
Which is now protected only by the remaining chinook.

The Siksestene people of the far north country,
Called the river home for years and Sixes was named,
For the Chinook jargon word 'sikhs,' meaning 'friend,'
Which was later interpreted as Sixes by gold miners.

In addition to the naturally spawning fish in this stream,
Roosevelt elk, spotted owls, and marbled murrelets,
Are commonly found roaming forests near the river,
Living freely in a still largely underpopulated region.

With the parallel running Elk River just north,
Sixes River enjoys little disturbance and remains,
One of the most pristine waterways in the entire country,
Where traces of gold can still be found in the black sands.

A beautiful sight to behold whether by boat,
Or along the banks observing as the sacred Sixes River,
Flows freely creating a natural environment for wildlife,
Passing through fields to a grand entrance at the Pacific.

Cape Kiwanda: Pacific City, OR

He loved the sea and all the surrounding waterways,
Of which he had plenty of options making his home,
Along the Nestucca River near the mouth of the Pacific,
Where he fished the rivers and sea sunup to sundown.

When the Fall Chinook Salmon entered the Nestucca,
He would be first to the rock well before daybreak,
And situated on his favorite spot for first cast,
Well before the fish boiled or sunrise touched the water.

Maris Spillane made home where the big fish lived,
And devoted his life to fishing all of Tillamook County.
When the seas were closed he would make his way,
To the Wilson River and catch fish naturally with a fly.

He spent most of his time in the spring and fall,
Along the Nestucca keeping tabs on the salmon run,
Often times the only man catching fish while others,
Just shook their heads in disbelief at his gentle touch.

He was a man whose convictions were often tempered,
By a wry sense of humor frequently making him the angst,
Of his fellow anglers though they admired his wittiness,
And desired his skill with a rod and reel in their own hands.

Though he ventured to the Little Nestucca on occasion,
And was often confused for a stump at Town Lake,
It was the Pacific Ocean he cherished and fished the most,
Pushing his dory boat off the beach to sea each morning.

Most often at daybreak he'd be found chest deep,
In the breaking waves beside his wooden dory boat,
Climbing into *Perseverance* to set out beyond Haystack,
Intent on filling the boat with albacore, chinook, and coho.

Whale watching and the scenery get most accolades,
And a climb to the top of Cape Kiwanda beats every view,
But it is Maris Spillane for whom the people speak of most,
Telling stories of the man and the many fish he caught.

He's a legend without a statue and an icon standing taller,
Even than the great natural landmarks in the region.
Spillane lives on through stories told in the community,
Of the original Dory Man and a fisherman to the core.

Cape Perpetua: Yachats, OR

Experience the Passion of St. Perpetua,
A land discovered by Captain James Cook,
During his voyages along the Pacific Coastline,
In search of a Northwest Passage through America.

Well before Captain Cook's discovery,
The Giant Spruce known as 'Silent Sentinel',
Began growing on the Cape and is nearly 600 years old,
With a circumference of 40' and over 185 feet tall.

The Silent Sentinel observed as Indigenous People,
Made their home nearby at the mouth of Cape Creek,
And still looked on after this land was their land,
When entire tribes were forcibly marched to this location.

The Giant Spruce has survived a 9.0 magnitude earthquake,
And subsequent tsunami at the Cape on January 27, 1700.
It lost its top during the Columbus Day Storm in 1962,
And even survived the great Christmas flood of 1964.

A forest of rich biodiversity with precious old growth,
Sitka spruce, Douglas-fir, hemlock, and surrounding flora,
Of breathtaking claytonia, trillium, and skunk cabbage.
Home to winter wren, spotted owl, and marbled murrelet.

Nearby Cooks Chasm formed from pounding waves,
Resulting in a foreshore lava cave that fills with water,
Then emerges upward through Spouting Horn's opening,
Akin to a whale's blowhole or a steaming ocean geyser.

Waves roll underneath Thor's Well filling from the bottom,
Until spouting violently upward then emptying once again,
Into what appears as a seemingly bottomless sinkhole,
That drains the entire Pacific Ocean to endless depths.

Towering trees loom over the headlands,
Disappearing in the heavy layers of coastal fog.
Frothy surf crashes gently upon jagged shores,
And coastal cliffs offer views for seventy miles.

The Alsea people called Halqaik home,
For 6,000 years living off the land and ocean.
Remaining piles of discarded mussel shells,
Are among the many reminders of their territory.

At night the nearby Heceta Head Light shines,
Eerily beaming 21 nautical miles from the Fresnal lens.
It is the most beautiful lighthouse along the Pacific,
Sitting hauntingly on a cleared cliff affront lush forest.

The Yachats River emerges at the foot of Klickitat,
Making its way west to the Pacific flowing through town,
Where the Yachats community rests on a cliff,
Overlooking the sea with rugged beauty in all directions.

Amanda De-Cuys: Yachats, OR

The whistling wind off the Pacific Ocean carries with it,
Stories and memories of our past and the haunting history,
Of this Oregon Coast region where Native People,
Were often captured and relocated by Government Issue.

Tall old growth Sitka Spruce densely bordering the trail,
Filters the ocean breeze and serves as an acute reminder.
On this trail it is far more important to listen and observe,
Than to risk underestimating this sacred and spiritual walk.

There were many years of battles and violent disputes,
Before an 1855 treaty promised a safe reservation,
With land, homes, and money where Native Americans,
Could live peaceably without disturbance from settlers.

Local Tribes agreed to cede their homes for a peace treaty,
Relocating to the Coast Indian Reservation's million acres.
But funds never arrived and without their hunting grounds,
Native People starved in large numbers before escaping.

The military was called upon to capture escapees,
And relocate Native People to Yachats internment camps,
With volunteer militias called 'exterminators' hunting,
Those fleeing the Reservation for a forceful return.

In 1864 Amanda De-Cuys was captured in Coos Bay,
Where she escaped and had been living with a settler.
She was forced to march over rugged coastal terrain,
Eighty long and craggy miles as the military pushed on.

Amanda was old, blind, and her feet tore open,
As she was forced to keep up on the rocky land.
Despite leaving enough blood on the trail to track her route,
She was dragged along against her will behind the militia.

Ten grueling days later the company arrived in Yachats,
And turned Amanda over to Indian Agents' custody,
Where she lived out the rest of her days in captivity,
Never seeing the Reservation fully dismantled or relocated.

Such a disturbingly dark history juxtaposed alongside,
Beautiful ocean scenery of the central Oregon Coastline.
A jaunt through the forest becomes a chilling reminder,
With Amanda's footprints permanently pressed in the path.

Coastal fog lingers in the trees with a repetitive lullaby,
Of crashing waves muffled by the forest canopy.
In a meditative and heartfelt expression of our ancestry,
Walk hand-in-hand with Amanda along the trail.

Acutely attentive to her story and the history of the region,
With gratitude for the preservation of her experience,
Providing opportunity to reflect in regretful sadness.
A sincerely solemn promise that history shall not repeat.

Charleston, OR

I moved out to that Charleston Harbor,
A temporary solution to my many problems.
Lured by the promise of a big paycheck,
A few months at sea then I'd leave for good.

Days were spent pulling in tuna, salmon, and ling cod,
Working the ship both day and night with hardly a meal.
We finally returned to port and to my disgruntled surprise,
They kept us unloading for hours before setting us free.

Then off we went to drink 'til daylight,
Continuing well after the taverns closed.
The sun came up and we were all sleeping,
Each of us ignoring the many calls from the captain.

We were content in the moment of freedom on land,
Knowing he'd be angry but would welcome us back,
To prepare the ship for another trip the next day,
Out to the ocean for our next long grueling test.

I planned to take my earnings and leave the port behind,
But the life of a seaman gets into your bones,
And the salt seeps into your blood and marrow,
Soon becoming a very part of your existence.

With the fresh ocean air in your lungs,
It's a challenge giving up a life at sea.
And although I lived alone in Charleston,
The town was welcoming and soon I had cohorts.

We were bad for one another and fed the contagious spirit.
When we were at port we would sneak from the law,
Got stoned along the seawall and nearly rolled a car.
We knew all the girls in town and had a tab at every bar.

I went to Charleston temporarily,
Just looking to make some money and leave quickly.
That was many years ago and it wouldn't matter anyhow,
Because I never could stay sober long enough to leave.

The town has a way of getting you drunk on the lifestyle.
Sitting on a high up bluff watching as the bridge is raised,
Observing large ships departing or returning to the marina,
And the sound of sea lions clamoring throughout the night.

Bright lights over the water illuminate the many ships,
Tied down each awaiting their next adventure to sea.
The stories Steinbeck would've written had he been here,
With plenty of fascinating characters readily available.

Charleston is a marvelous little town for the industrious,
Those looking to live closer to the land or create a new life.
An outdoorsman's dream with the flair of an artisan,
It becomes more difficult to leave the longer you stay.

Shore Acres State Park: Charleston, OR

If one thing can be said of Louis Jerome Simpson,
He had fine taste in the property he chose to purchase,
Including Cape Arago, Sunset Beach, and Shore Acres,
The latter of which became his home beginning in 1915.

Where the mansion and grand estate once stood,
There are remnants of what was once a tennis court,
With well-maintained formal and rose gardens,
An Oriental Garden, and the original Garden House.

A large Monterey Pine still stands on the grounds.
Initially planted around 1910 it has the honor of being,
The largest of its species in the entire country,
At 95 feet tall and with a circumference of 208 inches.

Perched atop rugged sandstone cliffs high above the ocean,
Crashing waves create a spectacle during coastal storms.
Gray whales pass nearby making a grand spectacle,
As they spout near the boats of commercial fishermen.

Miles of trails meander through damp forest,
Providing dramatic views at every opening and lookout,
As the path winds along cliffs connecting the three parks,
Making it easy to get lost in the beauty of this natural land.

Nearby Sunset Beach is aptly named for its scenic sunsets,
Where from the comfort of a car or with sand between toes,
The perfectly framed setting sun disappears into the ocean,
With silhouetted land mass and rising trees on each side.

So much to see within a compacted little slice of paradise.
With rugged ocean landscape and incredible views,
Shore Acres is undoubtedly the most productive scenery,
Along the entirety of Oregon's accessible coastline.

The Doerner Fir: Sitkum, OR

Driving down a bumpy dirt road –
In a beat up old red Subaru.

The heavy early morning fog –
Slowly gives way to the breaking sun.

Trees on the side of the road become visible –
And potholes are now avoidable.

The misty damp morning –
Still spreads moisture on the windshield.

Lost amid the dense and damp coastal climate –
Tall and sturdy conifers rise among thick greenery.

Rounding a narrow corner –
Splashing through deep ruts of muddy water.

Navigating a maze of logging trails –
Finding the beginning is most of the journey.

A half-mile crawl through unmaintained old growth –
The trail leads to a viewing platform at the base.

It is easy to become so lost as to not recognize –
But once discovered this tree is solely the best.

At 327 feet tall and 11.5 feet in diameter –
It is the tallest non-redwood tree on the planet.

Hidden deep in an old-growth stand in Coos County –
The 500-year-old giant is unmistakably resounding.

Superior to all others –
The Doerner Fir is King.

Joseph, OR

I will fight no more, forever.
The Wallowas are the very best.
Creating a pristine snowmelt lake,
And unrivaled peaceful quietude.

Tall peaks reach upward on the southern shore,
Guarding the glacier-carved Wallowa Lake,
Holding somewhere deep within its crevices,
The means to make a great roaring river.

The powerful kokanee rule these waters,
And grow up to seven pounds in size.
Non-anadromous as they are,
The fish get a healthy diet of zooplankton.

The true king of the lake is Wally.
A serpent monster known for settling tribal disputes,
And emerging periodically above the surface,
That dwells way down in the depths of these waters.

Rugged Wallowas with lush farmland below,
Bringing life to an otherwise barren landscape,
And luring artists to marvel in the beauty,
Of the Swiss Alps of North America.

The roaring Wallowa River gets its start,
Tucked away deep within the craggy rock of the slopes.
Upon close examination it is possible to see the moment,
Where snow and ice begin melting to form the stream.

Just as the snow melt river gathers momentum,
And finds width and depth in the lower elevation,
It emerges from behind the forest wall and enters,
Wallowa Lake beneath the shadow of the mountains.

Life springs from the bosom of the Wallowas,
Making the long snow-packed winter bearable,
By the abundance of spring prosperity and growing crops.
No better example of creating art from death than in nature.

The Wallowas: Joseph, OR

I walked away quietly.
Heading west, I think.
Toward the mountains,
Nonetheless.

It didn't much matter.
I could have been walking in any direction.
There were trees in the distance,
And I could already hear falling water.

I was heading out toward the hills –
To taste the freedom of the mountaineer,
Who knows the Universe,
Through Wilderness.

Upon arriving at a small clearing,
I set up a tent alongside the river.
Settling into the solitude of the mountains,
Listening to the drip of a nearby glacier.

Just before I wrote this poem,
I was standing outside my tent,
Admiring the Northeast Oregon night sky,
Illuminated by infinitely bright shining stars.

I was thinking about,
The remoteness of this mountain range,
And how solitude is the great motivator.
It is a necessary means for creativity.

'Nobody will ever read this poem,' I thought.
But the next one will be an improvement.
Because of this moment of isolation,
Chasing seclusion for the sake of inspiration.

I returned to the tent,
Put a log on the fire,
Scratched my scalp –
Stared at the blank notepad.

After thirty minutes,
I put my pen and pad aside,
Stepped outside the tent,
And took one final look at the Wallowas.

'Why even try to write?' I thought.
Nobody will ever create anything –
That can capture beauty such as this.
It is impossible to put these mountains into words.

As long as I should live,
This camp will not be forgotten.
It has become a part of me - and grown into me;
As I have grown into it.

It is not merely the photographs.
I leave part of myself here as well.
These mountains have consumed my being.
You just have to see them.

Metolius River: Camp Sherman, OR

Water seeps through porous rocks beneath Black Butte,
Where two groups of springs create the headwaters,
Of what becomes the west's most pristine and scenic river,
Flowing brief but brilliantly through old growth Ponderosa.

A scenic spring fed river that emerges instantly,
From the sacred grounds at Metolius Springs,
Near Camp Sherman with remarkable Mt. Jefferson views.
The stream flows northeast towards Lake Billy Chinook.

The Metolius River's glass-clear rise from dry ground,
Evolves to a dark cobalt blue in the shadows of fern green,
Then becomes azure and sapphire similar to Crater Lake,
In sunlight shimmer with a backdrop of burnt orange pine.

Bounded to the east by the forested basalt of Green Ridge,
West the slopes of Three Fingered Jack and Mt. Jefferson,
And settled in a treasured and forested pristine river valley,
The clear, cold, free flowing trout stream is like no other.

One of the west's most challenging dry fly fisheries,
With clear water, sparse cover, and multitude of hatches,
The river holds rainbow, bull, brown, and brook trout,
Along with the occasional kokanee salmon and white fish.

The name comes from the Warm Springs Sahaptin word,
'Mitula' meaning 'white salmon' referring to the Chinook.
Although the light-fleshed salmon namesake are gone,
Introduced kokanee salmon attract bear and bald eagles.

River otters and beaver can be found in and near the water,
With mule deer and elk in the surrounding forests.
Great blue heron, red-tailed hawk, and the often rare,
White-headed woodpecker are common at the Metolius.

A saunter along the banks reveals unique wildflowers,
Including western buttercup, bigleaf lupine, Tiger Lily,
And Peck's penstemon which is exclusive to the region,
Among tamaracks, alder, and many dense green firs.

A spellbinding river that fully captures the imagination,
The Metolius is a magically remarkable location,
That could be studied for a lifetime without understanding.
It keeps all senses engaged and tuned to its very existence.

Crater Lake: Klamath County, OR

Drive to the top of Mount Mazama,
Higher and higher to the peak.
Water below and the sun above,
A magnificent crescendo to the caldera.

The deepest and bluest fish bowl in America.
A bright cistern of pure rainwater and snowmelt,
Stored in a bottomless volcanic shell,
With tall cliffs leading down at all sides.

Standing on the rim be sure to locate,
The Old Man of the Lake.
An upright bobbing hickory log,
That floats by the winds and the tides.

Venture from the lodge trail to find,
The Lady of the Woods,
Seated in the nude and resting her head,
Against a volcanic boulder.

Scramble down to Cleetwood Cove,
A dream of Will. G. Steel come to reality.
Find a big rock along the shoreline to dive from,
And swim in the cleanest water in the world.

Be mindful of foot placement around the cliffs,
'Fore becoming another mysterious tragedy,
At the hands of the evil Llao.
Many have been claimed by the Klamath god.

The Klamath and Modoc Tribes,
Both avoided the mountain as it was known,
To invite death and lasting sorrow,
As home to dark spirits where people disappear.

Crater Lake formed in a battle between Skell and Llao,
Where in victory Skell cast Llao's limbs to the bottom,
And set the water animals to devour them.
Only the fish didn't and Llao emerged as Wizard Island.

Perhaps that explains the strange disappearances,
Such as Charles McCullars,
Who melted away while seated on a log,
With unbuttoned jeans in eight feet of snow.

Bigfoot looms large in this country,
And has been known to throw pinecones,
At pursuing rangers following his stench,
While tracking his steps through the snow.

Two Bigfoot have been killed at Crater Lake.
One was hit by a car and quickly whisked away,
By black suited government officials,
While the driver stood awestruck by her vehicle.

The second Bigfoot was hit by a train,
But conductors hid the body and didn't share the story,
Until after they reached retirement age,
For fear of being caught drinking on the job.

In the winter of 1997,
Military aircraft pursued UFO's,
Flying at low elevations above the lake,
Before a sonic boom was heard and they disappeared.

The mystery of Crater Lake is alluring,
And the beautiful landscape is so mesmerizing,
That a photographer could venture one step too far,
And tumble to the base of Llao's Island.

Hemlock Falls: Glide, OR

Lake in the Woods is akin to Sukhāvatī,
Hidden deep in the mountains of the Umpqua Forest.
And while many falls in the area are more dramatic,
Hemlock Falls captivates my imagination above all others.

The trail is located under overhanging trees near the lake,
And the discrete path provides a sense of discovery,
As the switchback descent leads through a forest of ferns,
Revealing fallen moss covered logs at the base of the falls.

Mankind has spent millions to create glorious cathedrals,
With high ceilings and expensive ornate details.
They build palaces of worship that contain the wisdom,
But could never accomplish what these falls provide.

Situated deep in old-growth forest with hemlock and fir,
Wildflowers and mushrooms growing in abundance,
And Hemlock Creek spilling over the edge quietly,
Twisting peacefully before splashing into a calm blue pool.

The mossy backdrop and thick vegetation of this oasis,
Creates a dramatic stage as water cascades in the forefront,
Reaching the idyllic constant decibel level for meditation,
Resulting in a therapeutic atmosphere for rest and solitude.

Hop across the perfectly placed dry rocks,
And make your way to the collection of large fallen trees.
Find one that rests at a 40 degree angle securely wedged,
Against the mass of many others at the base of the falls.

Rest your head on a fluffy moss pillow,
Close your eyes for respite or look up and watch,
As Hemlock Falls continues pouring quietly,
Into the glassy pool that surrounds beneath.

Hours of peaceful meditation can be completed,
In this magical location of forested solitude.
It is the great natural cathedral superior to all structures,
Where Zen Buddhism can be practiced in a natural setting.

North Umpqua: Glide, OR

I awoke beneath the cover of a tall Douglas-fir.
Reached for my knife and found it securely in place,
Stretched next to my shelter and tended to the small fire,
Before packing for another day near this glorious river.

The sun rose and I observed as the valley came to life,
With the morning fog lifting to reveal a sow and her cubs,
Drinking from the river with deer on the path above.
It didn't take long to appreciate this wild and remote forest.

With one last yawn and second big upward salute,
It was time to put some trail behind amid scenic mountains,
Traveling upstream on an amazing stretch of trail,
That borders the North Umpqua with astounding scenery.

The mighty North Umpqua roared beneath,
Ripping over sturdy rocks and graveled surfaces,
Later falling over cliffs in an unstoppable motion,
As the trail followed along winding through the forest.

Occasionally, I'd stop to spot a native steelhead,
Making its way through shallow and rippling waters,
Or using tenacity to propel over quick falling rapids,
Resiliently fighting to reach its spawning grounds.

The wild and scenic North Umpqua rumbled along,
Spilling from the western slopes of the Cascade Range,
Creating pure blue hints in mostly whitewater,
In some of the most remarkable land in the country.

As I made my way along the banks of the river,
On this journey to see the North Umpqua in its entirety,
I found that Steamboat was still the place for fishing,
And Mott Bridge remained after all these years.

On occasion a raft or kayak came passing through,
And I wondered if I was doing this trip all wrong,
Then I'd spot a fly fisherman on the other side,
And wade in myself knowing everything was right.

I stopped frequently to look at the canyon landscape,
The jade green rushing water, rock cliffs, and spires.
A mosaic of mountain meadows and hemlock,
Exposing unmistakable volcanic and geologic history.

An incredible 110 miles of waterfalls and tributaries,
The North Umpqua River provides endless opportunity,
And remote scenery unlike any other river in the region,
Best seen in twelve segments of the North Umpqua Trail.

Lemolo Falls: Umpqua National Forest

The tallest and most powerful along the North Umpqua.
Situated discretely in a peaceful green forested canyon,
Lemolo pours over a contorted cliff of columnar basalt,
Falling 165 feet into a moss covered rocky pool below.

Direct sunlight glistens off the misting reverberations,
Forming rainbows adjacent to the magnificent cascade,
Shining upon and illuminating the brightly colored green,
Of tangled vegetation that bilaterally frames the falls.

As the sun moves behind tall Douglas-firs above,
The falls become distinguished in the shadows.
The canyon wall turns dark green and the cascades,
Brilliantly glow in the changing light of the evening.

The valley is alive with a forest of flowers and ferns.
Nearby nesting osprey swoop through the mist,
Catching insects hovering carelessly in the cool spray,
And deer frequently carve their own trail to the river.

Slick moss covered rocks make the approach challenging,
Yet even from a distance the powerful bulk is astonishing,
With a wild and windward spray misting the valley,
Providing nourishment for the hillside vegetation.

The falls are still wild as the Chinook word suggests,
Although contained by Lemolo Lake Dam upstream.
The raucous monster stills put on quite a show,
During peak snowmelt when water explodes over the cliff.

The many roadside waterfalls of Umpqua National Forest,
Are tremendous sights to observe and should be cherished.
None are more rewarding than discovering Lemolo Falls,
An unmarked trail at the end of a bumpy dirt logging road.

Standing on the banks of one of Cascadia's greatest rivers,
In a lush green forest with the sound of a waterfall.
There is no better place to rest quietly on a stump,
Clearing the mind to the simple task of nothingness.

Gardiner, OR

Oregon is home to more ghost towns than any other state,
And each has a strange and unique history all its own.
Shaniko and Bayocean are two of the most fascinating,
But the community of Gardiner is intriguingly captivating.

On the north shore of the Umpqua River near Reedsport,
The town developed by accident when the *Bostonian,*
A schooner traveling up the Umpqua River for trade,
Wrecked in 1850 and its crew and cargo settled at the site.

With the ships merchant across country in Massachusetts,
The crew built and called the settlement Gardiner City,
Honoring the man who outfitted the ship in pursuit of gold,
Seeking the success of Robert Gray and John Jacob Astor.

Gardiner was a noted lumber port until a fire in 1880,
Then rebuilt with a new concentration around shipbuilding,
Becoming one of the busiest ports on the Oregon coast,
With ships sailing day and night up the Umpqua River.

The fascinating history of Gardiner is now overshadowed,
By nearby attractions like Dean Creek Elk Viewing Area.
A mosaic of pasture with woodland forest in the distance,
And a wetland sanctuary for waterfowl, birds, and beaver.

A herd of nearly one hundred Roosevelt elk live here,
Giving the sense of being in a famed national park,
With massive wild bull elk grazing in an idyllic meadow,
While simply at a rest area along Oregon backroads.

At Five Mile Road north of Gardiner along highway 101,
Views of the setting sun over the Pacific are bested,
By the lush green forest surrounding Tahkenitch Lake,
Creating intrigue with subtle glimpses through the trees.

Just south of Gardiner one of Conde McCullough's,
Many masterpieces stretches across the Umpqua River.
The Nationally Historic Bridge opened in 1936,
And is the last remaining swing span on Oregon highways.

So much of Cascadia can be missed unintentionally,
In the misguided pursuit of the final destination.
Town's like Gardiner can reveal unintended discoveries,
Like Jedediah Smith's campsite on the Umpqua shoreline.

Toketee Falls: Idleyld Park, OR

Perfectly framed by a columnar basalt formation,
The North Umpqua boils in a deep holding alcove,
Before making the plunge 85 feet into the tranquil pool,
Where clear water reflects the colors of the forest.

The sinuous gorge carved from lava flow,
And covered by dense damp moss and vegetation,
Creates an element of suspense and mystery,
As to what may be hidden behind the great wall.

Prior to the plunge water churns in buildup,
Generating power by sculpting an upstream pothole,
Inside a cylindrical crater beneath the water's surface,
Then pushes through the narrow gorge carved by millennia.

There is more to see beyond the lookout,
And down the backside of the viewing platform,
Ropes secured to stumps allow access to the lower pool,
Where the upward view gives perspective to the majesty.

The columnar wall is best appreciated from below,
Where the falls can be viewed in amphitheater fashion,
With full scope of the magnitude and shaping of the gorge,
Situated deep in the magnificent Umpqua National Forest.

Douglas-fir, big leaf maple, western red cedar,
And Pacific yew live together in harmony,
Along the banks of the North Umpqua River,
Creating a serene setting for the soothing waterfall.

Graceful as the Chinook name suggests,
Toketee Falls is an expression of poetry in motion,
As water elegantly and easily flows over the edge.
There may never be a more flawless waterfall.

Fall River: Deschutes National Forest

For Ken Seaverns

With net strapped across my back and fly rod in hand,
I walk quietly toward the stream the way he taught me.
Showing respect and appreciation for this magical place,
And giving thanks for the wisdom and lessons he shared.

Snow has not yet arrived and displays of autumnal colors,
Bring the soothing orange, brown, and red leaves that cling,
Holding on to the remaining spectacle of springtime,
Reflecting and drooping over peacefully clear water.

I recall fishing this spring-fed river in four feet of snow,
In the freeze of winter with snowshoes beneath gray skies.
Each with the child-like optimism that a fish may take,
While fully knowing they would be inactively subsurface.

Memories reemerge like the drift of an overused dry fly.
The 'Old Man and the Boy' sharing time on the water,
Cherishing the glory of an incredible spring river,
Grateful for a life spent in the woods simply casting.

This river is much more than water moving downhill.
For us, it is a sacred place and a religious experience,
The Fall River symbolizes enduring friendships,
Sharing a mutual affection for this extraordinary setting.

I don't make it there as often as I would like,
But found my way back to remember my old friend.
Reaching the trail's apex the gentle stream becomes visible,
Flowing quietly through the forest just as I remembered.

A welcome sight as I walked down the hill,
With slow deliberate steps to avoid rattling the earth.

Stillness abounds except the finch, sparrow, and towhee,
Chirping, playing, and enjoying life in the nearby trees.

Signs of wildlife are plentiful with markings in sight.
Including beaver activity in the bark of fallen trees,
Elk droppings regularly found along the banks,
And tracks from large predators preserved in dried mud.

This remote Cascades river is absolute perfection,
From its origins at the mossy and gurgling headwaters,
To the Fall River Falls and final release into the Deschutes.
Every twist, turn, and ripple of this water is awe-inspiring.

It is where I first discovered Buddhism and companionship,
And found Zen while seated on a riverside boulder,
Reading Gary Snyder with my senses attuned to nature,
Feeling most at home in this serenely beautiful place.

The river has massive rainbow trout that are plentiful,
And feed vigorously and truthfully to the hatch.
I would often find myself upstream near the headwaters,
Where brook trout play in deep holes beneath the current.

At times I would leave the fly rod behind in the car,
And simply go to the river to observe and listen.
With a pen and notepad sketching images of the forest,
Or inventing new words capable of describing this location.

The river has taken on a different meaning as of late,
With a newfound appreciation whenever I visit.
Remembering the man who is synonymous with Fall River,
And will forever encapsulate this remarkable stream.

Donner und Blitzen River: Voltage, OR

Thunder and Lightning along the steep canyon river,
Known simply as The Blitzen and draining Harney Basin,
Including Malheur National Wildlife Refuge and nearby,
Steens Mountain before ultimately filling Malheur Lake.

Flowing through marshland and glaciated canyons,
In the high desert where Eastern Oregon's diverse setting,
Results in the same river bringing life to wildflowers,
Thereafter turning to a dry rattlesnake infested terrain.

Running through arid country the river populates its shores,
With lush greenery and wildlife creating a natural oasis,
In an otherwise desolate and deprived portion of the state,
Ultimately forming wetlands where there is no outlet.

With Alvord Desert's modest seven inches of rain per year,
And two mountain ranges away from the Pacific Ocean,
The area receives very little rainfall forming a barren,
Dry, and cracked surface of arid desert amid the Northwest.

Rising from the lower slopes west of Steens Mountain,
The wild and scenic river flows north before turning east,
And passes near the small community of Frenchglen,
Prior to the picturesque canyon portion of its voyage.

15 million year old Steens Basalt is predominant,
With thin patches of rhyolite ash-flow tuffs appearing,
As the river runs through U-shaped glaciated canyons,
Which protect many petroglyphs of the Northern Paiute.

Nearby Steens Mountain reigns supreme over all matter,
As the largest fault block mountain in North America,
With well-defined escarpments, graben valleys,
And ice age glaciers that formed the rivers and canyons.

Riparian zones of the river feature willows, western birch,
Mountain alder, black cottonwood, and quaking aspen.
Seeps wetland communities and subalpine in the system,
Bring life to western juniper and mountain mahogany.

Mule deer, rocky mountain elk, and pronghorn antelope,
Are found along the river occasionally in various seasons.
American kestrels and great horned owl rule the sky,
With grouse, chukars, and valley quail living nearby.

The Donner und Blitzen is both thunder and lightning,
Marshland and desert juxtaposed in a barren landscape,
Creating incredibly dramatic canyons and a pristine river,
In a surprisingly underdeveloped region of the northwest.

Bigfoot on the Deschutes

Jackson County is home to the world's only Bigfoot Trap,
Designed specifically to capture the legendary hominid,
That dwells in forests throughout the Pacific Northwest,
And has been seen frequently in the State of Jefferson.

The trap was baited with carcasses for six years,
Only capturing occasional wayward bear,
Though it is still monitored by the Forest Service,
To potentially lure a curious Bigfoot into its confines.

Any true Oregonian has crossed paths with Bigfoot,
Whether directly or indirectly at some point in time,
And can share elaborate details of the experience,
Recounting particular smells, sounds, and memories.

I too have a fair share of Bigfoot stories to tell,
From many years of tromping through the woods.
The story to follow is factual based on experience,
As true as the still nervous fingers writing this tale.

I was out on the river,
As one is want to do,
A most peculiar little river,
With many twists and turns.

The water was shallow to see fish,
And the banks were fabricated with trees,
'Cept a few brief openings,
With high sandy beaches.

I was paddling upstream,
Drawn by the intrigue,
Of what might be lurking,
Just round the next bend.

Each new corner revealed to my eyes,
A fabulist new view of the mountains,
Disguised in the guile of white.
Mystery hidden within the terrain.

Round one bend and then another,
Peaking inside the lair of each volcanic cavern,
Curiously drifting by wondering what deceiver,
Might dwell inside such a cozy little den.

Round another bend I turned,
Revealing a new panorama,
When shock and awe became,
The great equivocator of truth.

Before me there stood,
Clear as day on a sandy beach,
The greatest deceiver of all,
A seven foot tall Bigfoot.

There before me the Bigfoot dove,
Head first into the water and wrestled,
A nine-foot sturgeon in a battle,
That lasted a full fifteen minutes.

When the Bigfoot emerged victorious,
He climbed out of the river with the fish,
Slung over his shoulder like a sack of potatoes,
Picked up a lava rock and belted the fish on the head.

In all my Bigfoot sightings I never once thought,
That he might like sturgeon for a meal,
But there he was preparing for dinner,
When a big black bear swam across the river.

The bear came stalking along the beach,
And as the Bigfoot turned to look up,
That ol' bear jumped on the biped's back,
And began pounding and clawing furiously.

Finally the Bigfoot had enough and ran away,
Retreating to the cover of the forest while the bear,
Enjoyed its newfound afternoon snack.
I sat mesmerized in my boat watching it all.

Just when I figured the ordeal was over,
And turned my boat to start heading home,
The Bigfoot came sprinting down the beach,
And tackled the bear right off the big sturgeon.

The two rolled through the sand and made a big splash,
As the battle resumed in the river with both creatures,
Clawing, growling, and shrieking horrendously,
Causing a chaos of commotion I couldn't fathom.

Each beast was fighting for their meal while I sat safely,
In my boat a mere 30 yards away watching it happen.
I wasn't sure how the battle would end but realized,
My stomach was growling and I hadn't caught a fish.

At this point being an innocent bystander,
Figured I deserved a good meal as much as anyone.
So I tied my boat up to a tree on the shoreline,
And waded in the water intent upon settling the fight.

State of Jefferson:

Here, sown by the Creator's hand,
　In serried ranks, the Redwoods stand;
　No other clime is honored so,
　No other lands their glory know.
The greatest of Earth's living forms,
　Tall conquerors that laugh at storms;
　Their challenge still unanswered rings,
　Through fifty centuries of kings.
This is their temple, vaulted high,
　And here we pause with reverent eye,
　With silent tongue and awe-struck soul;
　For here we sense life's proper goal.
To be like these, straight, true and fine,
　To make our world, like theirs, a shrine;
　Sink down, O traveler, on your knees,
　God stands before you in these trees.

　　　　　Joseph B. Strauss
　　　　　The Redwoods (1931)

Redwoods National Park: Orick, CA

Old as the Roman Empire,
And taller than the Statue of Liberty.
The Redwoods offer a glimpse at the past,
As they grow ever-taller into the future.

Some of the oldest and tallest trees on earth,
Many are over 2,000 years old and nearly 400 feet tall.
Although the forest is only 5 percent of what it was,
The remaining trees are outstanding marvels of the world.

The northernmost of coastal California,
Produces old growth redwoods, spruce, hemlock,
Douglas-fir, and a canopied understory properly protected,
The way we would a historically significant cathedral.

A mosaic of habitats including prairies filled with elk,
And oak woodlands rising in the foggy coastal climate.
Mighty rivers and streams flow along pristine coastline,
As gray whales pass resting sea lions, pelicans, and osprey.

Branches the size of cars and trees growing inside of trees,
With elevated root systems in the sky above,
Where the wandering salamander makes its home,
In the tall canopies of this lush forested ecosystem.

The redwood harbors burls of knobby growth at its base,
Where mass of stem tissue is stored and grows,
Creating a life system of the remarkable species,
To sprout a clone if tree falls or becomes damaged.

Situated alongside rocky and jagged coastline,
The redwoods have adapted to the harsh environment,
Growing salt-tolerant vegetation buffeted by salty winds,
Rising upward along the steep cliffs of the North Coast.

The last of California's naturally free-flowing rivers,
Smith River rises in the Siskiyou Mountains and flows,
Through the old growth redwood forests and prairies,
Providing respite for native salmon and steelhead.

Threatened wildlife including the tidewater goby,
Chinook salmon, spotted owl, and Stellers sea lion,
Are protected in the safety of the redwoods,
So they can stabilize and grow their numbers naturally.

Home to the Sequoia sempervirens,
The Hyperion tree is over 600 years old,
And at 379 feet it is the tallest tree in the entire world,
Growing modestly among many other Redwoods.

The Hyperion's size is only exceeded by legend.
Bigfoot is frequently spotted here,
Venturing across Highway 101 toward the beach,
Or sauntering through the woods among thick vegetation.

We should count ourselves lucky at the opportunity,
To stand beneath the Redwoods and look upward.
They very easily could have been decimated,
And their majesty is a reminder of our delicate ecosystem.

Battery Point Lighthouse: Crescent City, CA

Named for its crescent-shaped stretch of sandy beaches,
Crescent City is the gateway to California's Redwoods.
Home to one of the west coasts most distinct lighthouses,
With Battery Point Light situated atop a forested island.

Oil lamps were lit in 1856 at this California lighthouse,
A year after the ship *America* burned in the harbor.
Three salvaged cannons mounted on a nearby hillside,
Were fired regularly resulting in the name Battery Point.

The light survived the worst tsunami of the west coast,
When a massive earthquake struck Alaska in March 1964,
Sending waves crashing into Crescent City at 600mph,
Destroying buildings and boats but the lighthouse endured.

Battery Point Light allowed travelers to move about,
In a region of rugged mountains and unbridged rivers,
One time essential for the economic survival of the region,
So that sailors and fishermen could safely return to harbor.

The Cape Cod style lighthouse is home to jovial ghosts,
That playfully torment resident curators with mysteries,
Like turning off lights and modifying alarm clock settings.
Spirited pranks without any cause for serious concern.

Although the Fresnal lens was replaced by a 375mm lens,
The original is on display and the working lighthouse,
Illuminates the night sky offering private aid navigation.
It can be toured by those willing to wade in low tide.

Crossing 200 feet of rocks from mainland to the island,
With care and caution for potential sneaker waves.
Climb the staircase for a 360 degree light tower view,
Above the harbor, a fleet of ships, and the expansive sea.

Idaho:

"Ahead and to the west was our ranger station - and the mountains of Idaho, poems of geology stretching beyond any boundaries and seemingly even beyond the world."

Norman Maclean

Shoshone Falls: Twin Falls, ID

The Niagara of the West.
A wide series of waterfalls,
Pouring over the edge with grandeur,
Displaying the massive power of Snake River.

On a sunny day the crashing water,
Forms a series of rainbows around the falls,
And many more appear throughout the canyon,
Sometimes large enough to touch both sides of the river.

Looking downstream from the viewing platform,
The river disappears in a bend of the canyon walls,
Rolling along on its immense journey before emerging,
As the largest tributary of the Columbia River.

After a heavy rainfall or when upstream dams release,
Increased water levels in the Snake form a deafening roar,
Crashing forcefully over the cliff in turbulent fashion,
With the Shoshone producing an incredible spectacle.

At 900 feet wide and with 212 feet of falling water,
The magnitude of the falls is plenty dramatic,
Making the smaller complementary falls an afterthought.
Collectively the rushing water forms a massive collision.

The natural feature creates a barrier of fish migration,
Making the river below Shoshone a historic destination,
Where the Lemhi Shoshone depended upon the salmon,
And caught many here to sustain throughout the seasons.

Shoshone Falls and the Snake River,
An unstoppable force of powerful motion.
A climactic setting in the narrative of this great river,
Forming the most tremendous waterfall in all the west.

Payette Lake: McCall, ID

Camp Alice Pittenger in late fall.
I sneak away and shove a canoe,
To the farthest soil of Lucks Point,
Then push off into the water toward the other side.

From one point of Pilgrim Cove to the other,
Is barely a quarter mile by boat,
But nearly impossible by land in the night.
So I set sail with the Girl Scout camp in my sights.

Crossing the lake to meet the girl I love,
And roast marshmallows by the campfire.
Put my jacket over her shoulders,
And listen to the frogs croaking in the moonlight.

I'm greeted at the Pittenger camp boat dock,
As mature hands reach out to secure the canoe.
I look up to see that she has aged overnight,
And grown to adulthood just as I have.

She reaches out and pulls me onto the dock,
And we embrace much like we did many years before,
Sneaking away together on the banks of the Payette,
To share an hour or two in the moonlight before sunrise.

Not much has changed in the many years spent apart.
We still marvel at the expansive Milky Way,
Spread across the night sky and do our best to recall,
Scout knowledge by pointing out constellations in the sky.

Just a boy and a girl at camp twenty years later,
Making up for lost time on the shores of a distant lake.
Doing the same things we would have done back then,
If only there were more time before the morning bugles.

If this were summer camp it would be a risky endeavor,
Sneaking away to snuggle up under the stars,
While I show off my new fire making skills,
Roasting marshmallows on sticks carved from branches.

Since there are no nighttime curfews,
I left the borrowed canoe tied to the dock all night,
And we frolicked about carefree around the lake,
As we always wished to do on our summer camp trips.

We slept in late under the warmth of our sleeping bags,
And enjoyed the heat of a fire in the lakeside cabin.
We made our way around the lake catching fish,
And recalled many long forgotten scout skills.

Twenty years later a childhood reunion at last,
We rekindled our youthful love at the place it all began.
Doing things we could have only dreamed of as kids,
Finally exploring our summer sanctuary together at Payette.

Hells Canyon: Riggins, ID

Carved by the prodigious and renowned Snake River,
One of the most outstanding in all the west.
Hells Canyon is as impressive as the Grand Canyon,
And at 8,000 feet it is deeper and far less crowded.

With endless outdoor recreation opportunities,
The towering walls immensely above the water below,
Form the deepest river gorge in North America,
In some of the most remote land in the entire country.

The arid canyon hosts a variety of plants and animals,
With Rocky Mountain elk, bighorn sheep, and chukar,
Thinsepal monkeyflower and the rare Barton's raspberry,
All thriving in this desolate and arid environment.

The mighty Snake River is the twelfth largest in America,
And forms a natural border between Idaho and Oregon,
Ultimately creating the second deepest canyon,
With only Kings of the Sierra Nevada more profound.

The river hosts trout, steelhead, white sturgeon,
And the imperiled salmon as they move around dams,
Attempting to reach their spawning grounds,
Amid vast landscape with dramatic elevation changes.

This national showcase features scenic vistas,
That rival any on this continent and spectacular peaks,
Including the Seven Devils Mountains and He Devil,
Named for a vision of dancing devils seen by a lost Indian.

Home to the Nez Percé who grazed horses and cattle,
And left pictographs and petroglyphs on rock walls,
The region has remained sparsely populated over a century,
Since Chief Joseph's people were reluctantly pushed away.

Stand at the edge of windy steep cliffs looking down,
As the powerful Snake River appears miniscule below,
While observing towering peaks and rock-faced slopes,
Directly across the wide and expansive canyon rim.

Uninhabitable and vast remoteness creates a feeling,
Of being completely lost with many miles of desolation.
The breathtaking vistas, deep gorge, and quiet solitude,
Are magnificently unparalleled in this expansive canyon.

Wyoming:

"The Teton Mountains are, to my way of thinking, quite the grandest and most spectacular mountains I have ever seen... When viewed over the vast expanse of sagebrush which covers the valley, or with Jackson Lake and the marshes in the foreground, they present a picture of ever-changing beauty which is to me beyond compare."

John D. Rockefeller, Jr.

Grand Tetons: Jackson Hole, WY

What are men to rocks and mountains?
The Tetons must look down curiously,
At Ansel Adams setting up the perfect photo,
And people climbing all over the landscape.

Stand tall forever with your spectacular intricacies,
Keep your spires and cliffs watching over the valley below,
Look after the many creatures in your shadowed care,
And be sure that the Moose always has a place to roam.

Rise upward mighty mountains.
So that all others might look to you,
With equal parts wonder, awe, and disbelief,
Completely unsure if your beauty is reality.

Hold your snow long as you can.
Retain it in your crevices and valleys,
Even as the days grow longer,
And the world quickly warms.

Guard the fish in the lakes and streams below.
Keep them fed by mountain dwelling insects,
And sheltered beneath subalpine fir trees,
So they may swim freely in your natural waters.

Hold the Grizzly close within your bosom,
So she may rule this forest forever,
Raising cubs that only know the safety,
Of your caring and nourishing land.

Rise toward your jagged rocky crescendo.
The orchestra plays for you and you alone.
Woody Guthrie sings for an eternity,
Gratitude for the spectacular Grand Tetons.

Oxbow Bend: Moran, WY

The Grand Tetons are a masterpiece painting,
Where you can intimately study blemished brushstrokes,
Or step to the farthest wall and admire from a distance.
For the Tetons, Oxbow Bend is the preferred viewpoint.

With Mount Moran centered in the backdrop,
And the reflections of conifer forest on the surface.
Snake River carves its way around Oxbow Bend,
A wide and shallow horseshoe formed by gradual erosion.

From the western banks the sight is marvelous,
As Mount Moran mirrors on the surface of Snake River,
With a forested setting superimposed upon the water,
And the remarkable mountain range rising in the distance.

The most prosperous fishing river in all the West,
Holding native cutthroat, rainbow, and eager brown trout,
Motivated by the dry fly despite nearby eagle and osprey.
Grizzly, elk, and moose frequently drink from these waters.

The slow moving river moves peaceably,
As it enters Jackson Lake from the north,
Beneath the most glorious mountain range in Cascadia,
Featuring mystically surreal craggy peaks and spires.

Oxbow Bend holds suspense and anticipation,
For what it will reveal around the next turn,
And the exciting buildup never disappoints,
With intensely dramatic changes in the background.

An ever evolving scenery with revelations in the seasons.
Whether covered by snow or blooming in the spring,
The view at Oxbow Bend with Snake in the foreground,
Is inspiringly poetic with perfectly mesmerizing symmetry.

Cody, WY

Driving out of Yellowstone National Park,
Looking for a place to pull over and rest my tired body.
Casually attentive to the local radio station broadcast,
Discussing a man named Bill and his impact on the town.

They talked of him as if he passed away yesterday,
And this was their way of celebrating his legacy.
'Some small town politician,' I thought.
But it was Buffalo Bill Cody they were remembering.

A man who had been dead for a hundred years,
And in my mind was a mostly fictional old west character.
He was being recalled for his real life contributions,
In a town bearing his namesake and I had to learn more.

So I checked my wallet and figured I could justify a hotel,
If the price was right and had free internet for research.
Intent on learning about the incredible man who made,
A profound and lasting impact on this town and region.

In northwest Wyoming along the Shoshone River,
The Bighorn Basin is surrounded by mountain ranges,
Including the Absarokas, Owl Creek, and Bighorn,
And now serves as the west entrance to Yellowstone.

White settlement was restricted here until 1878,
Making this region one of the last frontiers to develop,
Until Cody first laid eyes on the basin from a lookout,
Atop Bighorn Mountains facing west over the valley.

Cody joined a group of Sheridan businessmen,
And began planning Cody Canal to bring water,
For ranchers to make a living in this new town,
Which was founded in 1896 and incorporated in 1901.

Buffalo Bill was undoubtedly the most famous American,
In the entire world and he was responsible for this town.
Building most of the infrastructure still in place today,
Starting with nothing but a flowing river and some land.

With some consideration I recognized that this man,
Was no longer being heralded for his legend and celebrity.
His foresight in the nearby outdoor recreation and tourism,
Resulted in the development and prosperity of this town.

Many years later the people of Cody remember Bill,
Not as the showman and entrepreneur of popular culture,
But as their neighbor, friend, and founder of their town,
Passing by on the street with a grin and tip of the cap.

Firehole River: Madison Junction, WY

Glassy clear water moves at near glacial speeds,
Amid rising steam as water boils underground,
Producing a warm fog that nearly hides the river,
Beneath the plumes of mist caused by erupting geysers.

Wildflowers grow along the grassy side of the river,
While stains of mineral marks decorate the other.
Bison stomp heavily in the damp soil at water's edge,
While the clear blue stream meanders through the meadow.

Firehole was aptly named by early trappers' observations,
That the steam makes the river appear as if it is on fire,
With smoke plumes rising upward over the fiery river,
Shallow and discretely hidden despite the low vegetation.

The Firehole flows through the Upper Geyser Basin,
Near Castle Geyser, Blue Star Spring, and Grand Geyser,
Where tourists walk single file along the plank to view,
The remarkable sights they have only seen in travel guides.

While the masses gather to gawk at nearby Old Faithful,
Just a short walk away there is silence and solitude found,
Along the vacant clear waters of the Firehole,
Where the only competition is grazing bison.

Geothermal features empty water into the Firehole,
Increasing temperatures and introducing,
Dissolved chemicals and minerals into the water,
Which does not impact the brown and rainbow trout.

Occasional fishermen will be found standing on the banks,
Where the river creates a quiet calm that lulls to restfulness,
Associating certain human qualities and attributes,
That fishermen will find rings true to their own mentality.

A spiritual location where elk and buffalo peacefully graze,
Keeping watchful eye while moving along the river's edge.
Live for a moment in peaceful harmony while sharing,
Wondrous scenery with mightily magnificent wildlife.

A mystical setting that seems almost otherworldly.
The Firehole and surrounding area is a surreal experience,
Putting senses in tune with the natural environment.
So much to observe in this ever-changing ecosystem.

Jackson, WY

In the Jackson Hole Valley situated between,
The Teton Mountain Range and the Gros Ventre Range,
There lies a remarkable town with incredible scenery,
An abundance of wildlife, and tremendous recreation.

Looking down from the peak of Taylor Mountain,
The town of Jackson appears beneath idyllic mountains,
Causing a thrill that is unmatched by any roller coaster,
As the road sharply declines downhill into the town.

Located just south of Grand Teton and Yellowstone,
Jackson is the perfect base camp for exploring the region,
With many historic buildings and unique shops,
On the outskirts of the most remarkable land in the country.

The Million Dollar Cowboy Bar in town square,
Is an iconic establishment of western history,
Much like the Wort Hotel and the Silver Dollar Bar,
Located near the famed antler arches in the heart of town.

The Hole is just a few miles west of the Continental Divide,
And welcomes the headwaters of the famed Snake River,
As water from highland mountain streams converge,
And join the river moving west through the valley.

Plenty of Elk and trophy deer find home in the valley,
With the National Elk Refuge located just north of town.
An abundance of bird species can be seen in trees,
Or flying along the winds of the clear blue Wyoming skies.

Jackson is the most perfect small town in the country,
With western history alongside outdoor adventure,
On the outskirts of the most amazing scenery in the west,
It is the idyllic place to settle before renowned exploration.

Montana:

"I am in love with Montana. For other states I have admiration, respect, recognition, even some affection, but with Montana it is love, and it's difficult to analyze love when you're in it."

John Steinbeck

Going to the Sun Road: Glacier National Park

The road climbs higher revealing breathtaking vistas,
Switchbacking upward toward the bright sun above.
Tall snow embankments border each side of the route,
With mountainous views and the deep valleys below.

Wildlife is abundant here and the frequently posted signs,
Warn that the bears are hungry and actively feeding.
A precautionary reminder that this area is wild,
In the remotely untamed landscape of northern Montana.

Lake McDonald casts a perfect reflection of the mountains,
Including Mt. Vaught, Cannon Mountain, Mt. Edwards,
Mount Brown and a prominent series of others,
Precisely overlaid upon the clear glacial lake.

Each and every rock in Lake McDonald is distinct,
And the colors are a magnificent sampling of the brightest,
Reds, greens, blues, pinks, and yellows under the water.
A beautiful subterranean variegate of colorful rocks.

McDonald Creek flows into the lake with fallen logs,
Crossing and covering in a tangled and jumbled mess.
The gentle stream flows through the forest channel,
Providing spawning grounds and a shaded retreat for fish.

The Grizzly is ever present in Glacier and its large tracks,
Can be found alongside scratch-marks and fur left on trees.
It is frequently seen prowling in the lively forest,
In search of berries and the occasional creek dwelling trout.

Glacier's historical ice age produced over 700 lakes,
Forming the headwaters of the Continental Divide,
Where a single drop of water could be split in two,
With each arriving separately at the Pacific and Atlantic.

Over 1,100 plant species exist in the coniferous forest,
Including beargrass, monkeyflower, glacier lily, fireweed,
Balsamroot, Indian paintbrush, and Englemann spruce,
As well as Douglas-fir, limber pine, and western larch.

Nearly all the historically known plant and animal species,
Still thrive in this completely intact alpine ecosystem.
Glacier is home to 71 mammal species of all sizes,
Protected by the expansive wilderness areas since 1910.

Covering every terrain in the park along the 50 mile drive,
Going to the Sun reveals glacial lakes and cedar forests,
Windswept tundra atop the pass and scenic viewpoints,
Found at every turn along the crown of the continent.

Garden of One Thousand Buddha's: Arlee, MT

Situated in the Flathead Indian Reservation,
Is a pilgrimage destination and place of worship,
For people of all faiths and spiritual backgrounds,
On ten acres of carefully groomed green gardens.

Snowcapped mountains surround the Jocko Valley,
Where Gochen Tulka Sang-ngag Rinpoche's guidance,
Has led to a garden that inspires Buddhist ideals,
Of joy, wisdom, compassion, and enlightenment.

The footpath is designed in the shape of the dharmachakra,
Representing the teachings of the Buddha through design,
Particularly the Noble Eightfold and the cycle of life.
The route to liberation from samsara on the Buddhist path.

As a form of mandala the trail represents existence,
Composed of an outer ring with eight symmetrical lines,
All stemming from the central figure of Yum Chenmo,
Great Mother of Transcendent Wisdom and compassion.

The Buddha's represent the thousand avatars,
Who are destined to redeem the world in successive eras,
And will be born in our religious age accordingly,
With Guatama Buddha only the fourth in this kalpa.

The Garden is a place to cultivate inner peace,
And unite all faiths to generate profound merit,
Reducing global negatives and promoting lasting peace.
A place where spiritual practices are welcome to all.

To some it may seem a trivial roadside attraction,
On the road to Yellowstone or Glacier National Park.
It is a beautifully peaceful place of enlightenment,
And a microcosm for what this world could become.

Flathead Lake: Polson, MT

Glacier carved knife ridges and sharp craggy peaks,
Thousands of years of erosion whittled Flathead Valley,
Forming the sprawling jewel of Flathead Lake,
Situated at the base of the Swan and Mission ranges.

It is a fine sheet of water with an abundance of wildlife.
None more than at Wild Horse Island which features,
Plentiful bird species, bighorn sheep, coyotes, and bears,
With bald eagles frequently flying overhead hunting fish.

One animal reigns supreme in Flathead Country,
The mysterious but distinctly observable Flessie.
A mostly docile lake creature that survived the ice age,
And lives in the depths of the great lake of the west.

The legend originates with the Kutenai,
The first native tribe to live on the lake,
Making their home on the forested island for safety,
Then traveling in all directions by way of canoes.

One winter day two girls crossing the lake toward camp,
Saw a pair of antlers protruding from the icy surface.
They attempted to cut the antlers free as a souvenir,
Until the ice began shaking and a monster appeared.

Flessie wreaked havoc on the Kutenai,
Nearly decimating the tribe until only a few remained.
After the incident the tribe fished only near the island,
Rarely venturing out into the open waters of the lake.

In 1889 Captain James Kerr of the steamboat *U.S. Grant*,
And his hundred passengers observed a whale-like creature.
A passenger shot at the monster but was unable to kill it.
Flessie swam for safety in an escape that spurred a legend.

Local residents refer to the lake monster as Flessie,
And the creature is reported several times each year,
With the majority of citizens claiming to have seen it,
And a spike of thirteen verified reports in 1993 alone.

Descriptions of the monster are generally consistent.
Eel-shaped with a long body of 20-40' and brownish skin.
Steel-black eyes and body like a whale or a large sturgeon,
Reported earnestly and covered seriously by local papers.

The Leviathan hides deep beneath the clear glacial water,
And reportedly torments fishermen by swimming circles,
Creating waves and currents in the water around boats,
Large enough to rock even the sturdiest of lake vessels.

Though some legends may seem entirely implausible,
There is some science supporting Flessie's existence.
75 million years ago the Flathead area was an inland sea,
And an aquatic reptile could have survived the ice age.

It is the largest freshwater lake west of the Mississippi,
And is deeper than the Yellow Sea and Persian Gulf,
Which means that the lakes' vastness could support,
A massive supernatural creature such as Flessie.

Sightings should be reported directly to Laney Hazel,
A Montana Fisheries Biologist and former skipper,
Who has worked on the lake nearly sixty years,
And tracked reports of Flessie for over thirty years.

The validity of Flessie is still unverified,
But the magnificence of Northwest Montana,
A remnant of Lake Missoula with superb mountain views,
Is a remote and remarkable sight well worth the visit.

Missoula, MT

Closed for the season.
Try golf, bocce ball, or pickle ball.
The rivers are closed and John Maclean is gone,
You have come too late and missed the heyday.

This town isn't what it seems.
The rivers aren't what they were and fishing is dead.
Trade in your fly rod for a used tennis racket,
And find a new hobby because this isn't the place.

The town of mythical fly fishing from the esteemed book,
Of a family's deep ties to Missoula and Little Blackfoot,
Is entirely unrealistic and as unbelievable as lake monsters.
Don't buy into fiction and save yourself disappointment.

Use your money and take the family somewhere tropical.
Go on that golfing trip you have always dreamed about.
Take care of home improvement projects you neglected.
But for the love of God do not go to Missoula.

It is too far out in the middle of nowhere,
And makes no sense why anyone would ever visit.
There's no major commerce or bustling cities,
The rivers and guides aren't as advertised so stay away.

Missoula was once an unknown paradise for fly fishermen,
But it isn't any more so take your fly rod elsewhere,
To the storage unit or a nearby thrift shop preferably.
Just know it won't be useful if you make it to Missoula.

As for me, I'll situate at the confluence,
Of four of the of the most pristine major trout streams,
Where there are hundreds of miles of remarkable rivers,
And the views are as incredible as the surplus of fish.

We are Cascadia

The mythical land of Cascadia.
A region defined by its geography,
Geology, topography, and many massive forces,
That shape and form magical beauty all around.

The national holiday occurs every May 18th,
As a visceral reminder of the dynamism of the region,
And in remembrance of the day that Mount St. Helens,
Erupted and violently shook Cascadia in 1980.

With a flag of Blue, Green, and White,
Representing the ocean, rivers, forests, clouds, and snow.
A symbol for the natural beauty and inspiration,
That the Pacific Northwest bioregion provides.

A lone-standing Douglas-fir placed front and center,
The flag signifies endurance, defiance, and resilience.
All the symbols of the Cascadia Flag come together,
Representing everything that it means being Cascadian.

A region defined by the Fraser and Columbia watersheds,
Rivers flowing into the Pacific from Alaska to California,
Along the coastline through the temperate rainforest zone,
And inland to the continental divide at Idaho and Montana.

Founded on connections to environmentalism,
Bioregionalism, privacy, civil liberties, and freedom,
Regional integration, local food, and economies.
Cascadia is a bioregion of shared ideology and lifestyle.

Originally the Oregon Country and Columbia District,
Thomas Jefferson, John Adams, and John Jacob Astor,
Envisioned the territory as a free and independent empire,
Self-ruling fur traders on the western side of the continent.

In the land of falling waters natural integrity blends,
And sociocultural unity defines Cascadia as a region,
With culture and ideological identity as the common bond,
Unifying people and land for all citizens of the bioregion.

We are Cascadians and thrive in the locality of our region,
Where water falls, trees grow tall beside rivers and lakes,
And mountain peaks provide the backdrop in most places,
With clear starry skies and sunsets over the Pacific Ocean.

55743528R00066

Made in the USA
Middletown, DE
21 July 2019